Owen Blayney Cole

The Midnight Ride,

An Irish Legend Dramatised, with Christmas and New-Year Carols, etc.

Owen Blayney Cole

The Midnight Ride,
An Irish Legend Dramatised, with Christmas and New-Year Carols, etc.

ISBN/EAN: 9783744729239

Printed in Europe, USA, Canada, Australia, Japan

Cover: Foto ©Andreas Hilbeck / pixelio.de

More available books at **www.hansebooks.com**

THE MIDNIGHT RIDE,

AN IRISH LEGEND DRAMATISED,

WITH CHRISTMAS & NEW-YEAR CAROLS,

&c.

BY

OWEN BLAYNEY COLE.

Post equitem sedet atra cura.

HOR. III. i. 40.

PORTISHEAD.

MDCCCLXXXVI.

CONTENTS.

PROLOGUE TO THE MIDNIGHT RIDE.

In this little drama I have, as in several previous compositions, mostly in the ballad form, endeavoured to perpetuate in verse local or family legends, grains gleaned from the parental acres, deeming the sheaves containing such better worth my threshing out than those of foreign growth; though, failing the former, the latter are not by any means to be rejected. For the legend here dramatised I am indebted to the late Rev. Alexander Ross, Rector of Banagher, in the county of Londonderry, Ireland, whose guest I was so long ago as the year 1831, when of a summer day I would direct my steps up the glen of the waterfall, where was a thorn garlanded with the offerings of votaries, suggesting by anticipation (for the picture was not yet painted) Sir Frederick Burton's *chef d'œuvre*, "The Blind Girl at the Holy Well." It is scarcely necessary to say that Dungiven Castle, the ruins of which [then partially existed, is greatly magnified as to its importance in the scenic poem.

DRAMATIS PERSONÆ.

CAREW, SIR GEORGE, The Lord of the Castle.

BERESFORD, Brother of Lady Carew.

KNOX, Chaplain of the Castle.

CAMPBELL, A young Scottish Chieftain.

OGILBY, Seneschal of the Castle.

DONALD, The Warder.

MACARTHY, A Celtic Chieftain.

LADY CAREW.

ROSA, Her Daughter.

CANARA, Sister of Macarthy.

MORLACA, A Sennachie, or Prophetess.

Time—morning, noon, afternoon, evening, and midnight of the same day.

Era—about the year 1599.

The Midnight Ride.

SCENE I.

(The bell-tower of Dungiven Castle, Londonderry, Ireland. Early morning.)

OGILBY.

WHILE clambering these steps the thought arose,
Whereabouts now the lady whom we saw
Departing on her hazardous emprise
Some two months since ; should she be fortunate,
As 'tis my prayer she may, 'tis nearly time
That thy long silent bell her welcome sound,
Winner of the brave race for house and lands.

DONALD.

But for thy presence here as visitant
My watch-tower would be as a dungeon, worse :
For they who are imprison'd take no thought
Save for themselves, regardless of the world
Without, from responsibility exempt ;
Whilst I, with none to aid me, must defend
This castle from the accident of fire
Or greater danger that awaits us oft
From the retainers of Macarthy, men
Cruel as wild cats, sighted in the dark
To catch a mouse ; but we can bell the cat,
Else would it matter little whether won
Or lost the wager, from conspiracies
Safe neither way.

OGILBY.

Aye, luckless are the odds :
For even should her Ladyship attain

To Essex, the Lord Deputy, her request
Free to refuse, even should she find her way
Thither on palfrey, might not her first gains
Result in loss? himself incapable
Of any base malevolent design,
Might not some caitiff of Macarthy's clan
Without recourse to open violence
Confront the traveller at Pellipar *
So that she be belated ?—a month since
She had been here but for an accident.
'Tis now St. Lammas Eve, if she should fail
Ere midnight at the castle gate to knock
The wager will be lost.

DONALD.

True, 'tis the latest date ;
But may she not, exempt from accident,
By such impediment have been delay'd,
As most besets the great, the law's constraint ?
Under the highest many the degrees,
Each an impediment ; yet win she must.
Is not our Lady gifted with the wand,
The snow-white wand that in her hand she bears †
The knotted whip instead ? Was e'er such show
As when our Lady on her palfrey black
Quitted the court-yard, to the iron hoofs
Resounding, sweeter music than of bells ?
Clad in her purple riding robe enlac'd
With gold, on her fair shoulders a snake chain,
And on her head a plumèd coronal
Starr'd with an emerald, she looked the form
Of victory. Let men in England prate
Of their Godiva and her Peeping Tom,
The Lady of Dungiven be my toast.

* Pellipar, near Dungiven, now a country seat.
† As in Moore's Irish melody, " Rich and rare," &c.

OGILBY.

And mine, meriting most our feälty ;
Veil'd our first mother when from Paradise
Departing, and she went afoot, unlike
Our lady, of the saddle capable.
Nor heeding to be hidden from the view ;
Of dignified demeanour, in her pride
Is no presumption, though not Scottish born,
Like some of us whose parentage lies north *
Nearest the head, not distant from the heart,
Is our good lady.

DONALD.

By her energy
Making amends for her lord's quietude,
Who soldier though he be would stay at home
Rather than ride save with the cavalry
As their commander ; Rosa after him
Takes more than after her, beauty except ;
To the Macarthy wed, heal'd were the feud
Betwixt the families, such headlong race
Again preventing.

OGILBY.

Not so —the gage lost
Not thus would she regain her heritage :
Her heart belongs to Campbell, trust my word
'Tis Campbell not Macarthy wins the Rose.
But now must I betake me up Glenshane
Thither as her attendant bid—Farewell.

[*Exeunt.*

* The Scotch settlement in Derry is here anticipated, it was not until the
following reign that Derry became Londonderry.

SCENE II.

(The Glen of the Serpent among the mountains of the Slieve Gallion range, near Banagher. Time—noon.)

ROSA.

'Twas at thy summons, Morlaca, I came,
Hoping thy promis'd aid in hour of need,
Trustful yet hesitating, threading the glen
Precipitously gloomy, but for growth
Of various foliage that o'ercanopies
The stream ; tended by Ogilby, who yon
Awaits conclusion of our conference.
Hither I come, a maiden half forlorn,
Thee visiting in thy sequester'd cell
Saintly enshrin'd : yet dost thou seem akin
To the mysterious being that, 'tis said,
Haunts, prison'd here, the watery element,
Pent in the grotto of the cataract,
The reservoir by crevices supplied
From the tremendous precipice : how mute
The pool, how loud the torrent, contrast strange
Of calm and tempest, peace and strife ! This thorn
With ribbons garlanded that simulate
The aureola of Iris smiling yon ;
This stunted thorn wet from the cataract
Attests the healing virtues of the well,
Just tribute to the snake medicinal
That cures infirmities of sight,—many
The votaries : but not to lave mine eyes.
My outward orbs, that shrink not from the ray,
Come I to thee, 'twas by thy promise led
To read the mirror of the waterfall,
The glassy book oracular. I come
Trusting mid the delineated forms
Therein descried, to thee intelligible,
Expert in auguries, I may some tidings
Hear of my mother.

MORLACA.

Who should now return,
Having been absent the allotted term.
Such tidings as are mine to give be thine.
But ere we vex the mirror, on this couch
Of moss reclining 'neath o'ershadowing boughs,
List of the Saint and Serpent while I tell,
That thou may'st not depart in ignorance
Of that which coming hither thou shouldst know.
—Long ages since when holy Patrick preached
The wrong requiting by the serpent done
To our first parents, this glen, far remote
From the apostle, was inhabited
By a huge snake, voluminous with scales
That glitt'ring as he glided in the sun
Showed like a burning city, being dangerous
When from the hills the hoarded icicles
Dissolved in floods inundulating the vale
And plains beyond ; with men and cattle thus
His maw he fed, by his tempestuous tail
The crops destroying and their tenements.
With anguish'd tears the desolated folk
Besought O'Heeney,* saint to Patrick dear,
Who dwelt at Banagher, with gifts and prayers,
To interpose in their extremity.
Not deaf to their petition, with his staff,
Gift of St. Patrick, fatal to the toad
And reptiles all of species venomous,
The serpent was arrested, and in rings
Concentrical revolving, settled down
In small circumference of this crystal font
Bright with the molten silver of his scales,
And with his quicken'd soul intelligent,
Restoring sight, and to the dubious mind
Giving to fathom the invisible,

* St. O'Heeney, otherwise St. Owen. Banagher, a village near Dungiven,
not the Banagher on the Shannon.

Deep sounding as the serpent of the sea
Whereof 'twas spawn'd : hence is it that this pool
Is fraught with blessings like that sacred sign,
The Brazen Serpent of the wilderness,
Or Siloam's basin by an angel stirr'd.
But coupled with the metamorphosis
Was this strange covenant, whether by saint
Ordain'd or serpent mystery remains ;
Though for the sphinx more suitable than saint,
Being enigmatic :—'twas this : After years
A thousand the first lady in the land
Nearest to where the miracle was wrought
Should ride a thousand miles betwixt the Feast
Of Pentecost and Lammas, and that blood
Should stain her palfrey's fetlocks : 'tis now time
For the fulfilment of the oracle ;
And for thy better knowledge list the rune ;

    After a thousand years have pass'd
    Since the serpent's scales were cast,
    The lady of the land must ride
    'Twixt Pentecost and Lammas tide
    A thousand miles—for years a mile
    Islands twain to reconcile,
    And her horse's hoofs be red
    With the blood at midnight shed.
    At fulfilment of the gage
    Lost and won a heritage.

ROSA.

So marvellous a legend ne'er was said
Or sung in prose or verse : this canticle
Quaint though it be disquiets me yet more
Breathing of bloodshed : terrify me not
With such presentiments ; to thee
Come I for consolation, not alarm.
Yet of the serpent would I make a friend,

Clasping him to my bosom, by the coils
Acquiring knowledge, not of evil but good,
So might I of my mother's safety learn.

MORLACA.

Was e'er such duteous daughter! safe arriv'd,
Thy mother having ridden a thousand miles
Alone or aided, will the prize resign
To Rosa and her lover:—chide me not—
Hush, 'tis the auspicious moment; the warm sun
Has to the centre climb'd of the blue vault—
But not for thee to gaze into the pool;
Too delicate thy limbs for the rough floor
Framing the lucid mirror, and thy sight
Untaught to read the mystic characters
By the initiate scarcely legible,
Might suffer injury requiring cure,
Whereto prevention is preferable.
Myself alone descending to the marge
On bended knees will question the abyss.
Follow not thou, await me by the thorn.

(*Morlaca retires to the pool, from whence after an interval she
returns.*)

ROSA.

What hast thou witness'd? Is my mother safe,
And has she prosper'd in her enterprise?

MORLACA.

Not yet has Lady Carew reached the gate
Of Purgatory, region in thy creed
Unmapt, she lives, nor is her scarlet coat
With travel stain'd or changeful atmosphere.
Already has she passed the battlements
Of Derry, and before to-morrow morn
Will have embrac'd thee, accident except.

16

ROSA.

And is my mother veil'd from evil eye
Of jealously which all unknown to thee
Is said to tempt thy kindred?

MORLACA.

In yon well
Shrin'd Truth, nor may I cheat the oracle
Concealing half; truth in her nakedness
Most beautiful scant drapery requires
Disparaging—thy mother though secure,
Behind her rides a noble cavalier
From whom she would continually escape
As from the darkness.

ROSA.

Yet more would I learn.
Is the pursuer of thy race or mine,
Celtic or Saxon?

MORLACA.

By his sword and mantle,
Tann'd boots voluminous, and haughty mien,
He might be deem'd a Spanish cavalier.
Yet of Milesians have I known the like.

(Ogilby now stepping forward conducts Rosa homewards through the glen.)

SCENE III.

(The castle-hall—afternoon of the same day.)

BERESFORD.

STRANGE tidings these, Sir George, which from Coleraine
Arriv'd in haste I bring ; in the offing yon
Rides a galleon which by her lofty stern,
Gilded and carv'd, may be another bird
5 Of the Armada's feather; feigning trade,
'Tis stow'd, they say, with wine of Xeres rare,
Her freight rank treason, contraband of war,
Both crew and captain with the Spaniard leagued,
Ocampo the confederate of O'Niel.*

CAREW.

Dangerous news, but my intelligence
Surpasses thine ; Earl Essex has resign'd,
And in his stead reigns Mountjoy, now Vice-King.
Nay, interrupt me not, more is there yet to tell.
Never before was such a desperate race
As that by Devereux run ; soon as the Earl
Had certain intimation from the Queen
Of her displeasure, how that by his fault
Ocampo with the rebels had combin'd,
O'Neil abetting, reinforcements spite
From England sent at her own regal cost.
Soon as these plaints to Essex were conveyed,
Her anger to avert, and in her grace
Himself to reinstate, hot-foot he went
O'er stormy waves and unexpected roads
Arriving at the presence, resolute
Himself to exculpate, before the queen
Prostrate he knelt ; with haggard countenance,
Unkempt his love-locks, negligent his dress,

---

* Here again a paranomasia ; Ocampo's sphere of action was in the south of Ireland, where embarking at Kinsale he was taken prisoner by Mountjoy, and obliged to quit the kingdom.

How chang'd from him, the gallant Devereux
To Leicester scarce inferior in renown
(Himself once fain to bend the suppliant knee,
Unbid returning from the Netherlands,
Where he miscarried, e'en as Essex here).
'Twas thus beholding Devereux at her feet,
The royal breast to pity was inclin'd.
This the result : the queen by him surpris'd
In her dishevell'd charms—the rumour such,
Her frown relaxing, after conference held
With Burghley and Sir Francis Walsingham,
Acquitted Devereux of deliberate wrong,
And sends us Mountjoy as his substitute.

KNOX.

Being chaplain of the castle, mundane things
Not much concern me; more my thoughts incline
Towards her who doth exemplify the text,
Though in a race run all, one wins the prize.*
But not of Isthmian or Olympic dust
Speaks holy Paul, save as by allegory ;
'Tis of the heavenly race, whereto compar'd
All else is retrograde—yet do my prayers
Follow our Lady dear, steadfast in faith,
Who forth hath ventur'd in a righteous cause.
Of her have tidings come ?

CAREW.

No news as yet
Save from the solar herald, whose red rays
Predict a bright to-morrow when the bars
That would prevent the rising shall be broken.
To-night the moon is in her plenitude,
Smiling upon a hopeful enterprise
Plann'd by a lady vindicating rights

* 1 Cor. ix. 24.

Peculiar to her sex: three ways, methinks,
There be of doing things; by head or heart,
Or dexterous hand auxiliary to both.
The three combin'd are best.

KNOX.

Perplexities
Must oft by contradictories be met.
To many shifting winds the mariner
Shapes his adventurous course; wanting the voice
That stilled the waters of Gennesaret.

CAMPBELL.

With thee, Sir George, the strong hand gauntleted
Holds foremost place, controlling head and heart;
Be mine the heart, though for the iron hand
Need is there, doubtless, on occasion fit.

CAREW.

Not much amiss thou speakest, my young friend,
E'en as becomes thy quality and race,
That like the thistle of thy native hills
None may encounter with impunity.
Symbol not here quite inappropriate—
This castle mine more by inheritance
Than by alliance with the Beresfords
Has not been held without exchange of blows
Ourselves betwixt and naturals of the soil,
Whose antiquated title to excel
Must be obtain'd a charter from the queen
Or representing her, the deputy,
Which to secure remonstrances despite
My Lady hath set forth ambassador.

KNOX.

Prudence may over violence prevail.
Be wise as serpents, harmless as the dove,

Saith Scripture, and from Flaccus we may learn
How force devoid of counsel harms itself,*
Precipitated by its senseless weight
To the abyss, by our antagonists
Better exemplified than by ourselves.

[*Exeunt.*

SCENE IV.

*(A ruinous church on the sandy shore of the stream flowing from
the Glen of the Serpent, and not far from the castle.)*

CANARA.

UNHEEDING consequences hither have I come
To this dismantled church founded erewhile
By St. O'Heeney when by miracle
He quelled the snake yonder umbrageous glen
Frequenting, so tradition saith : not this
Our first encounter here, but 'tis the last,
For us no future.

CAMPBELL.

The future who can tell,
Save those the orbits of the sleepless stars
Who calculate :—the present time is proof
Both to the past and future ; by its use
The past may be aton'd, the future blest.
But why this boding tone ? Why should we part
Never to meet again ?

CANARA.

Our paths diverge—
Thine is with flowers enamell'd, thorny mine.

* Vis consilii expers mole ruit suâ.—HOR. III. iv. 66.

Another loves thee, Archibald--one born
To make thee happy, not unfortunate
As were thy lot united unto him
Whose parentage is a rebuke to thine—
Saxon usurpers of our heritage ;
Of whom art thou though guiltless of offence
Intentional ; this the stern lesson taught
By those to whom our tutelage belongs,
E'en from the altar preached by holy priests
Who blessing us curse those without the Church.

CAMPBELL.

But what if, Canara, I could disprove
Their doctrine, what an' I could demonstrate
By history, than legendary lore
Less dubious, that our Caledonian clans
And the Hibernian are of kindred stock,
Both branches of the apostolic vine
By the Culdees transplanted from the East.
Scots both !—if this to thee I can make plain,
Would'st thou not stoop, hoping to reconcile
The threads by discord sever'd ? List to me
Preceptor of a pupil yet untaught
Save how to wound by beautiful disdain.
Turn not away those glances that most charm
When scornful. List, a thousand years ago
In the sixth century :—nay, hear me out.
The time is pass'd and can no more offend—
A thousand years ago, in the sixth century
Reigned Cabra Ruada, surnam'd the Red,
Grandson of Con, hero of hundred fights.
Thron'd in the northern province of this isle
Amid the wooded hills of Donegal ;
His aid to supplicate came fugitives
From Caledon, ambassadors elect
Of the despairing monarch of the Picts
By Scandinavian Vikings overpower'd.

The Caledonian prince to reinstate
Sailed the three sons of Ruada renown'd—
Again that scornful smile : nay, hear me out,
Dalriads were they and Christians; by their aid
From Norsemen freed was Albany, so call'd,
Whom to requite for their heroic deeds
On each of the three Dalriads was bestow'd
A Caledonian spouse with regal dower,
So that the Caledonians Scots became.
From whom derive the Campbells of the clan
Diarmid, known as children of the Mist.
Thus, Canara, have I prov'd we are akin
And owe each other love.

CANARA.

Such love, indeed,
As sister owes to brother, owe I to thee.
Be thou as brother ! more endearing ties
If such there are, which well may be denied,
To me are interdicted as to thee :
Of the church catholic am I, by thine
Calumniated as of Babylon.
Hast thou not heard such heresy from Knox,
The castle chaplain, who shall thee unite
With Rosa, thine already, if my heart
Reads hers aright : in conquering her hand
Me hast thou for auxiliary, convinc'd
That by such wedlock all may yet end well.
Thus fondly would I compensate the love,
The words of love that ne'er may be renew'd
Twixt thee and me ; far better for us both
They never had been spoken :—part we now
No more to meet.

CAMPBELL.

Oh, say not so, or yet
If part we must, resume thy haughty mien,

Nor break my heart by insincerity.
Why should we part? hush, we are not alone.
Seest thou yon kerle, who with malignant scowl
Controls our movements? Is he of thy house
Or an invidious spy? 'Twas only now
His dangerous swarthy features caught my sight.
Him had I known observant, my discourse
Had been less audible, but thee my words
Could never harm.

CANARA.

'Tis Fergus, gallowglass,
The henchman of Macarthy who awaits
To be my escort homewards : fear him not
Even had he heard thee, in the Saxon speech
Wholly unlearn'd he could not comprehend.
Since the departure of my brother, absent still
I scarce know why unless it be to quench
The hopeless passion smould'ring in his breast,
By the Confessor deem'd heretical,
By me calamitous ; e'er since he went
Fergus has been my squire importunate,
Now beckoning me impatient of delay.
Yet ere we part, if parting cost thee pain,
To my poor presence if inclin'd :—to-night
Know that by Rosa to the castle bid
Again we meet.

CAMPBELL.

Merciful words—
Let come what will, a tutelary star,
Thou never canst be distant from my sight.

[*Exeunt.*

SCENE V.

(Midnight and moonlight. The castle bell announces the approach of Lady Carew. Fergus, the gallowglass, concealed in the shadow of the archway stabs Macarthy, mistaking him for Lady Carew.)

CANARA.

My BROTHER, oh, my brother, lift thy head,
Speak to me ere the torrent of thy blood
Have borne me with thee to the silent tomb.

MACARTHY.

Dying the wager I have won—to Rosa
My love till now unspoken I bequeath.

(He dies.)

KNOX.

His days are ended, his life's youthful race
Completed ere arriving at the goal
Where should have been renewal of his might!
Now may the castle tocsin be attun'd
To dying knell.

BERESFORD.

Where is the homicide?
The doer of this felon deed, where is he?
And what his motive? he cannot be of ours.

OGILBY.

'Tis Fergus, gallowglass of him he slew,
Who would have slain another, even her
The Lady of the castle deem'd the bar,
So he imagined in his ignorance,
Most villainous, to his chieftain's rights.
First in the race Macarthy by the arch
O'ershadow'd met th' assassin's vengeful pike

Falling as at the sacrificial shrine
Instead of her sav'd by angelic hand.
Thus may the passage be interpreted,
The caitiff who would doom anticipate
Fast have we bound, no language hath the wretch
To us intelligible, but in his looks
Is that which dungeon dark doth best beseem.

(The scene here changes from the court-yard to the great hall of the castle.)

LADY CAREW.

Silent save for my anguish, even now
Scarce am I able to find utterance,
My joy is chang'd to grief, knowing too late
By whom accompanied I would escape,
Fearful to cast an anxious look behind,
Lest Orpheus-like failing of my emprise
My purpose should in disappointment end.
Alas for him my rash competitor
Who me o'ertaking even at the goal,
Dying hath turn'd my triumph to defeat,
Penalty paying that would have been mine,
But for Macarthy whose disastrous love
Hath oft disquieted me.   Where is Rosa ?

CAREW.

Gone with Canara,
Sister to slain Macarthy; gone with her
To help her weep.

BERESFORD.

No better comforter.
Honour and votive tears are tribute due
To the Macarthy.   But now that thou art safe,
My sister, and again in thy own home,
Forgetting for awhile this ghastly deed,

Wilt of thy wondrous quest give the result ;
Hast thou achiev'd thy purpose ?

LADY CAREW.

Yea and No !
This parchment scroll sign'd by Elizabeth
And pictur'd with her royal frontispiece,
This grant of lands in perpetuity *
Reads now as a death warrant.

BERESFORD.

By the queen
If sign'd, seal'd, and deliver'd, treason 'twere
The document to question, and the death
Of the competitor, no longer such,
Doth more enhance the price—a soldier speaks—
Nor yet uncharitably, had he speech
Whose lips are clos'd for ever, his discourse
Would doubtless show that to defend the cause
Of womanhood he trod the path believ'd
Most chivalrous.

CAREW.

This blood hath countervail'd
The tidings of Ocampo's overthrow ;
The wily Spaniard counting on the aid
Of Hugh O'Neil, Tyrone's rebellious Earl,
Whose force was intercepted by Mountjoy
Now captive taken, must depart the coast,
His ransom paid.   How had we all rejoic'd
At this success of the Lord Deputy,
But for mischance of this eventful night.
(Re-enter Canara with Rosa.)

* Royal grants of land in Ireland formerly bore the portrait of the reigning sovereign. I have seen such among my own family parchments and else where.—O.B.C.

27

CAMPBELL.

Sad meeting this, too strangely terrible—
Scarce dare I now approach thee, Canara,
Yet would I comfort speak : is there no balm,
No sweet alleviation in the thought
That he is honour'd as thyself belov'd,
That with thee dwells the sympathies of all !

CANARA.

If balm there be alleviating pain,
'Tis in the consciousness that by the fate
Of him the object more of fear than love,
The bar is broken parting thee and thee,
Rosa from Archibald, betrothed by death
Of him the winner of the heavenly race.

(Canara joins the hands of Rosa and Campbell in the presence of the other persons of the drama.)

[CURTAIN.]

₊ "After all my researches I cannot authenticate the history of one of our finest specimens of architecture, that of the old church of Banagher. Built of cut freestone in a good and even elegant style ; some modern characters engraven on the west door date its foundation A.D. 477, which needs other evidence. Beside the church stands the monastery, the only remaining one in the country—it is entire except the roof."—SAMPSON'S LONDONDERRY.

Christmas Carols.

I.

THE lark that to the sunny skies
   Uplifts its rapid wing,
Cuckoo that to itself replies
   When welcoming the spring;
Nor other bird the woods among
Of Philomel can match the song.

The Day with its external glare,
   Its vanities and shows,
Can never with the Night compare,
   That more brings than repose,
Peopling the palaces of gloom
With forms of visionary bloom.

Far sweeter than of Philomel,
   Melodious refrain
Was by shepherds heard of Israel
   A new nocturnal strain;
By them were beauteous forms beheld
Poetic visions that excelled.

Of what those shepherds saw and heard
   In land of Palestine
We come to tell, unto our word,
   Good people, all incline;
Though chill the air the strain hath charm
Of hoary age the heart to warm.

Beneath the shelter of a rock
  Reclin'd the shepherds lay,
No other thought except their flock
  To guard from wolves had they,
Unless, perchance, in Scripture taught,
Of Him that was to come they thought.

Yet scarce did those poor peasants deem
  That they of low degree
Should be included in the scheme,
  That theirs the first to see
The child who should the curse retrieve,
The wrong requiting done to Eve.

To them reclining on the grass
  An angel bright appeared,
Not knowing how it came to pass
  Of him were they afear'd,
Until the silence thus he broke—
Was ne'er such voice as his who spoke!

"Fear not," the angel said to them,
  "To you this happy morn,
In David's city, Bethlehem,
  The Prince of Peace is born ;
And this to you shall be for sign,
A manger doth the babe enshrine.

"Good tidings of great joy I bring
  To you and all the world."
E'en as he said their radiant wing
  The seraphim unfurled ;
And ere to heaven they reäscend
Their voices thus in chorus blend

"Glory be to God above,
   Enthron'd o'er highest height ;
To men who dwell on earth be Love,
   Wherein He doth delight."
This carol heard from year to year
Again we sing your hearts to cheer.

II.

Two Books there be, two wondrous books—
   The sacred, the profane ;
And none prevailed in former time
   To reconcile the twain,
Until from heaven an angel came
The joyful tidings to proclaim.

How war the Titans waged with Jove
   The cyclic poets told ;
How Danai and Dardans fought,
   By Homer was enroll'd,
Ended Virgilian epic lay
At dawning of the gospel day.

'Twas now that in Judæan mead,
   Where shepherds watched their fleece,
To them glad tidings were reveal'd
   Of universal peace ;
To them was open'd wide a page
At distance view'd by Syrian Mage.

The Book of the Evangelist,
  Which Sinai's doth excel,
Reflected may we now behold
  In glass of Raphaël.
More precious than a diadem
The Book that tells of Bethlehem.*

For the New Year.

I.

OF thy progenitors, New Year,
  Full many have we known,
Now dubious whether with a cheer
  To greet thee or a groan,
The latter the alternative,
Unless thy parent we forgive.

Forgive we may, but scarce forget
  The disappointments dire,
The various causes of regret
  Bequeath'd us by thy sire;
The brave Crusaders slain, whose fame
Serves only to augment our blame.

The heroes at the water brinks
  Eager their thirst to assuage,
Tempted by the Egyptian sphinx
  To treacherous Mirage;
Such ills who strove not to prevent
Merits not praise but punishment.

In allusion to Raphael's "Madonna degl' Ansidei" purchased for the
National Gallery.

Hence is it that we hesitate
    At the coming to rejoice
Of one impos'd on us by fate,
    Regardless of our choice ;
Since unsolicited our vote,
Why waste on welcoming a groat !

Thus mused a grey-beard anchorite
    Awaiting midnight stroke,
When suddenly a Phantom bright
    Appearing thus outspoke :
" Why is thy countenance so sad ?
Oh, look on me and be thou glad !

" Dost thou lament the brave who shed
    Their blood in the Soudan,
Heroes the scymetars who fed
    Of the fierce Musselman ?
Of him the martyr of Kartoum
Would'st thou avenge the cruel doom ?

" Know that their names are now enroll'd
    'Mongst those escap'd the strife,
Who quaff from cup of beaten gold
    Beneath the Tree of Life
The water of that crystal well
Surpassing Eden's Hiddekel.

" For all things is a time confest,
    'Vails not the past to chide ;
Look forwards, ever hope the best,
    In Providence confide ;
So shalt thou welcome with good cheer
As heretofore the coming year."

Thus saying, a pictorial shower
  Scatt'ring, the Phantom went,
E'en as the bells from the church tower
  Announced the new event,
Replacing him aboard on Styx, '
Eighteen Hundred and Eighty-Six.

II.

A RUGGED nurse hath the New Year,
  January her name,
Yet not averse to social cheer
  The reputable dame.
With quip and crank and merry wile
Expert the infant to beguile.

Not long will she retain her place,
  No sooner born than bred,
This gouvernante the youth will chase,
  Impatient to be wed ;
Of Spring enamour'd to her bower,
He hastes at blossoming of flower.

Expiring in his loving arms,
  Brief space hath he for tears,
Comes Summer with her riper charms
  And passion that endears,
Quick'ning the pulses of his heart,
Alas, that they should ever part!

Yet such the ordinance of fate,
　Widow'd again he wooes,
In Autumn finding next a mate
　Whom he again must lose ;
But not before to soothe his grief,
Enrich'd is he with cereal sheaf.

So oft in matrimony tried
　Still doth its ties engage,
In Winter now he finds a bride
　Adapted to his age ;
Wedded to her for life and death,
To her his heir he will bequeath.

Winter.

Der Winter steigt, ein Riesenschwan, hernieder.
ANASTASIUS GRUN.

WINTER, a giant swan with wings unfurl'd,
Descending gradual whitens the wide world,
He sings no song, seems it as though his mood
'Twere only on the slumb'ring seeds to brood,
Till spring that on his breast finding repose,
Thence draws the nutriment whereby she grows;
Soon will a thousand flowers their bloom display,
A thousand song-birds wake the sweet love lay.

Another Swan there is, the angel Death,
Brooding upon the seeds the sod beneath,
Silent and solemn far extends his power,
None knoweth of his coming day or hour.
The grass-green grave, the ossuary blest,
Alike he cherishes unto his breast ;
The while we watch and pray, until the spring
The flowers and fruits of Paradise shall bring.

An Evening Landscape.

Goldner schein deckt den Hain.—MATTHISON.

GOLDEN shine decks the pine,
In the grove the leafy glimmer
Grows continually dimmer.

Calm the wave forgets to rave,
Tow'rds the isle with swan-like motion
Glides a pinnace from the ocean.

Yellow sand streaks the strand,
Clouds now white, now red as roses,
Horizen of the West discloses.

To and fro the rushes throw
Their arms as 'twere a welcome flinging
To the wild fowl yonder winging.

On the height the anchorite,
The ivy-mantled belfry's warden,
Tends his myrtle-tinted garden.

O'er the stream dies the gleam,
Already is the vale forsaken,
By the shadows overtaken.

Silver shine bathes the pine,
From heroic graves ascending
Myths are with the moonbeams blending.

36

Nænia.

Auch das Schöne muss sterben, das Menschen und Götte bezwinget!—SCHILLER.

E'EN the Beautiful must die, Death is the portion of mortals ;
　Ne'er doth brazen heart melt of the Stygian Jove.
Once and once only, by Love beguil'd, he relented ;
　But, on the threshold recall'd, Orpheus again lost his bride.
Strove Aphrodite in vain to save her darling Adonis,
　Viewing his delicate limbs torn by th' infuriate boar.
Thetis, herself divine, failed her godlike son to recover
　When at the Scæan gate, falling, his doom he fulfilled ;
Yet from the flood arising sad with the daughters of Nereus,
　Greatest of heroes for him sounded funereal dirge.
Hence may we learn that the Gods are not unconscious of sorrow,
　When the excellent die, seen never more on the earth.
Thus it becomes us mortals to mourn for the good and heroic,
　While unto Orcus their home songless th' ignoble descend.

The Sonnet.

Zwei Reime heiſs' ich viermal kehren wieder.—A. W. SCHLEGL.

FOUR rhymes within my compass I contain,
These rhymes distributed in such a way
That one assume of couplets the array,
Each interpos'd betwixt an outer twain;
Then of the fourfold strophe lest the chain
Should exercise too arbitrary sway
Over the fancy, checking its free play
Changes the cadence to a triple strain.
—Him would I ne'er with laurel garland grace,
Who thinks to measure by its mere extent
My worth, nor knows that deepest mysteries
May be conceal'd in limitary space;
Symmetrical my form, and I present
Truths with advantage of antithesis.

The Water-Lily and the Swan.

Die stille Wasserrose steigt aus dem blauen See.—GEIBEL.

THE gentle Water-Lily that in the lake doth grow,
Its moist leaves softly quiver, its cup is white as snow,
The moon when she arises with beams to fill it up,
The treasures of her radiance will empty in that cup.

A swan towards the Lily is crossing the blue lake,
The snow-white swan is singing its farewell food to take.
It sings so sadly, sweetly, in singing 'twill expire,
Oh, lily, water-lily, didst thou that song inspire !

From Afar.

Diese Rose pfluck' ich hier in der fremden Ferne.—LENAU.

THESE roses that I've gather'd in a foreign garden here
How gladly would I bring to thee, oh, Lady fair,
Yet miles many interposing, soon faded were the bloom—
Love ne'er from love should sever beyond a flower's perfume,
No farther than the nightingale to chambers of the West
Can carry mossy filaments to decorate its nest.

Farewell of the Princes of Powis.

THERE is one Almighty power, one supreme above all thrones,
One exalted only Ruler who all earthly kingdoms owns ;
By Him kings and princes govern, in His gift is every crown,
He it is that lifts up nations from the dust and casts them down.

Now the crown is leaving Cambria where it has for ages been,
But fond liberty smiles on us as the azure sky serene,
Though dark clouds around may gather while His blessings crown
 the land,
What can humbled Wales do better than leave all in His hand !

Merlin's Reply to the Farewell.

BRAVELY princes have ye spoken while the humble knee was bent,
Him confessing who of nations doth the rise and fall prevent ;
Though the sun withhold his splendour, ne'er forsaken is the year,
Soon the roses and the lilies after winter reappear.

Of Cambria, though the harp be shatter'd, silent ne'er the song of
 bard,
And the heroes slain in battle shall not fail of their reward.
From the country of the vanquish'd shall be nam'd proud Albion's
 heir,
And to earth's remotest regions Cambria's prowess shall declare.

The Mostyn Harp.

THIS silver harp excels th' Homeric shield,
Stain'd is the buckler oft with drops of gore ;
Few would desire Pelides' brand to wield,
Or bend the bow Odysseus twanged of yore.
But even now this harp has power to charm
As in the glorious days of good Queen Bess,
Whose gracious proclamation freed from harm
The loyal Bard who should its chords caress.
E'en such the lyre that Taliessin woke,
Cadwallon, Modred, and pindaric Gray,
Whose minstrelsy the cloud of error broke,
Concealing Cambria's mountains from the ray.
—Long as the Harp of Mostyn shall endure
Wild Wales of royal favour is secure.

*₊*The silver harp inherited by the Mostyns from their ancestors is the
subject of a letter from Queen Elizabeth (dated October 23, 1568—in the 9th
year of her reign) sanctioning "in our Marchesses of Wales" its use as against
the vagrants naming themselves "Minstrels, Rhythmers, or Barths."

www.ingramcontent.com/pod-product-compliance
Lightning Source LLC
Chambersburg PA
CBHW061238260626
47172CB00003B/907